THE HORSEBACK LIBRARIANS

Jane Yolen   illustrated by Alexandra Badiu

Albert Whitman & Company
Chicago, Illinois

The sun is barely poking its head over the horizon. A young woman on a tan horse called Sand, saddlebags packed full of surprises, has already begun her rounds. She is delivering books to readers in the backwoods of Kentucky.

The roads are often broken, potholed. Paths overgrown.

Some trails have been destroyed recently by gully washers.
Some families have had to leave their homes without warning.

The horseback librarian takes it all in stride.

So does Sand.

The first night, Anna Mary—"rhymes with library," she likes to say—shelters in a small forest of pines. She ties Sand to one of the trees, then snuggles into a sleeping bag.

It is too nice a night to set up her tent.

In the morning Anna Mary eats a quick meal of cornbread and has a cup of tea she has heated on a small fire.

Before they leave, she makes sure the fire is put out, the ashes scattered with dirt.
Then she takes Sand to a nearby creek, where he can drink water and munch grass.

Then they set out again.

"There she is!" Adam cries, looking out the window to the dirt track that winds around the meadow.

"Of course," says his mother as she pumps fresh water into the sink to wash the breakfast dishes. "Has Anna Mary ever missed a visit?"

"Anna Mary, rhymes with library!" Adam shouts as he runs out to greet her.
She lets him lead Sand to their barn.

Inside the house, Anna Mary shows Adam the two books she has picked for him: *Andy and the Lion* by James Daugherty and *Abraham Lincoln* by Ingri and Edgar Parin d'Aulaire.

"They are about two brave men," she tells him, knowing his father is away at war.

Anna Mary stays through lunch, having read *Andy and the Lion* with Adam and gossiped a bit with his mother.

Then, with three hard-boiled eggs Adam's mother has given her, Anna Mary leaves for her next visit.

"Can you see her yet?" asks Alice, still in bed though she is no longer spotty with measles. "Anna Mary?"

Her mother smiles. "Rhymes with library?"

She checks once again, looking down the dirt road that leads—after a rough mile— to where her husband works. "Not yet," she says as Alice sinks back onto her pillow.

Soon enough, Anna Mary is there. She has *Alice in Wonderland*, and Wanda Gag's *Millions of Cats*, because Alice is allergic to cats but loves them in books.

"Not that she is ready to read it, though you could read it to her—her namesake book." Anna Mary knows Alice's mother can read, though she rarely does. It should be a treat for them both.

Anna Mary begins reading the story to the two of them as dinner is prepared.

Anna Mary stays overnight in their barn. And she is lucky to be there, with a brief, hard rain shower in the middle of the night.

In the morning, the road ahead is muddy as Anna Mary and Sand leave
the barn, having eaten one of the eggs from Adam's mother for breakfast.

But the sun is now up, full and golden.

"When will she be here?" cries Susan, waving her hand to get her teacher's attention.

Mrs. McDougal turns from the blackboard. It is Friday, and she is weary, as she always is at week's end, but never too weary to answer a question.

Susan's hand goes down, and for the next hour she concentrates on her arithmetic.

Anna Mary, rhymes with library, arrives just in time to share the school lunch. She is carrying a heavy saddlebag filled with books for each one of the seven children in the school.

Susan's book is a fairy tale collection by the Brothers Grimm, with bright illustrations. She doesn't even take time to see what anyone else has received. She looks at the first illustration. It is a princess in a long gown, a crown on her head. Susan sighs and begins to read.

There is even a book for the teacher, about Paris, France. A place she has never been.

After the children go home for the day, Anna Mary and the teacher make dinner together, because the school is also the teacher's house.

There is a bed in a separate room for Anna Mary. She will sleep well tonight. As will her horse, in the schoolhouse barn with a bale of hay and water in a stall.

Without all those heavy books, the trip home will be easier.

Anna Mary reads long into the night, a book she has saved for herself, called *Emily Dickinson's Poems*. It is a good book she has never read before by a poet she has barely heard of. It keeps her up until midnight by the schoolhouse clock. And this, for Anna Mary, is the reason she is a librarian. This love of books, of words, of stories, and of poems that tell the deep truth.

Author's Note

The Pack Horse Library Project was part of a larger US government plan called the Works Progress Administration, or WPA, started in 1935 during the Great Depression, giving jobs to millions of unemployed people. This project delivered books to remote regions in the Appalachian Mountains, a large system of mountains in the eastern US. My late husband and his three brothers were born and brought up in Webster Springs, West Virginia, a small mountain town, and my husband mentioned this story to me years ago. Though this was a Kentucky project, it had fascinated him. He and two of his brothers were big readers, and three of the four became teachers like their parents. The mostly women librarians serving their communities this way had various titles: book ladies, packsaddle librarians, book women, and book riders, among others. They usually rode on their own—or rented—horses and mules. At least one walked with books in a backpack.

The project included thirty different libraries and employed around two hundred people. They reached around one hundred thousand Kentucky residents, either at their homes or by bringing books to local schoolhouses. Anna Mary (rhymes with library) is not a real person but a combination of all those wonderful book riders who helped keep the love of books, words, and the truth alive along the back roads of the southern Appalachians during the Depression.

To all my librarian friends, and to the Stemple Family—JY

For my parents, who let me be who I am—AB

Library of Congress Cataloging-in-Publication data is on file with the publisher.

Text copyright © 2023 by Jane Yolen

Illustrations copyright © 2023 by Albert Whitman & Company

Illustrations by Alexandra Badiu

First published in the United States of America in 2023 by Albert Whitman & Company

ISBN 978-0-8075-6291-8 (hardcover)

ISBN 978-0-8075-6292-5 (ebook)

Printed in China

10 9 8 7 6 5 4 3 2 1 WKT 26 25 24 23 22

Design by Mary Freelove

For more information about Albert Whitman & Company,
visit our website at www.albertwhitman.com.